The Quiet Place

Sarah Stewart

Pictures by David Small

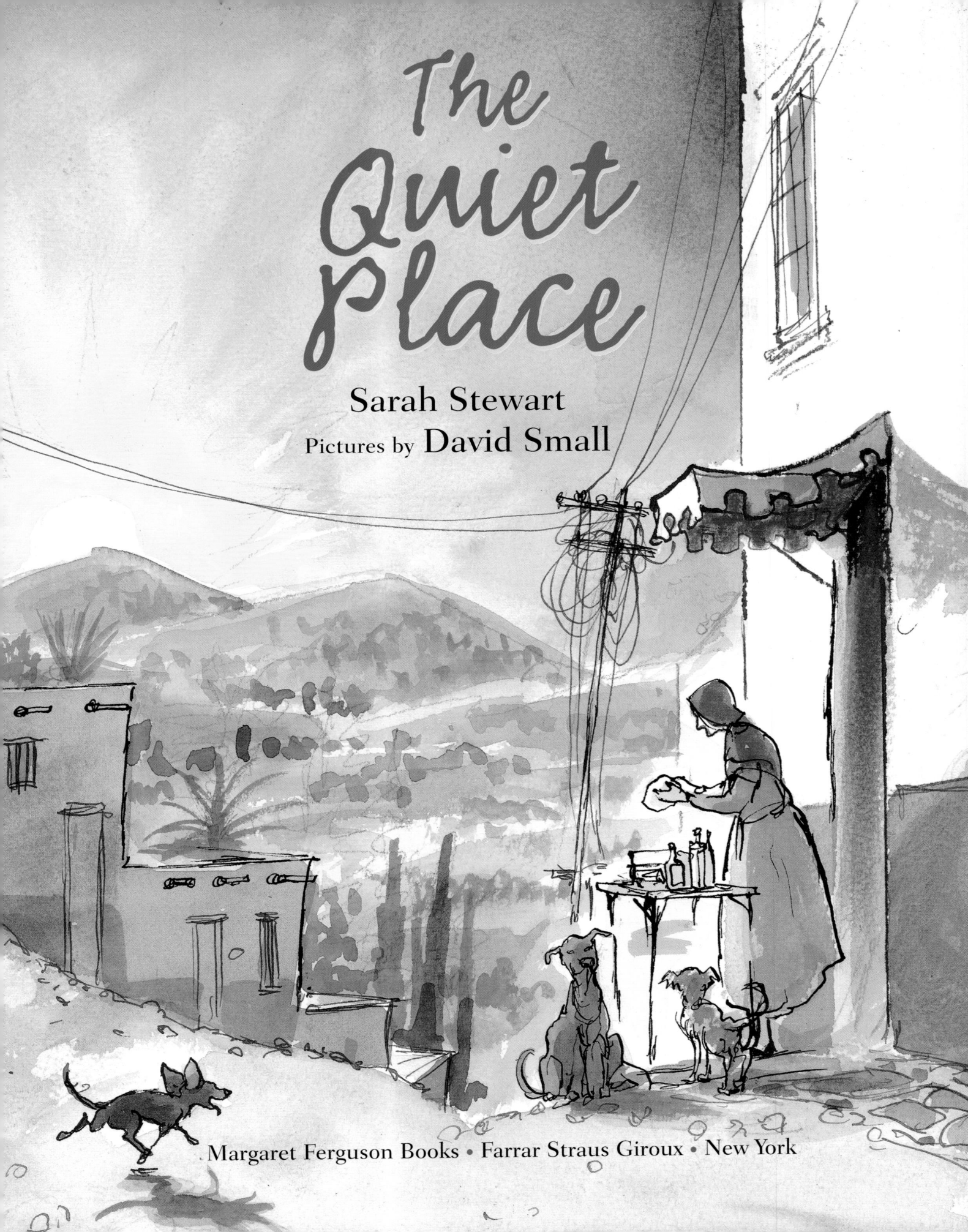

Margaret Ferguson Books · Farrar Straus Giroux · New York

April 5, 1957

Dear Auntie Lupita,

Here is my first letter in English. I am going to practice my new language by writing to you. Thank you for your letter in Spanish. It was so easy to read! I remember most of the English words you taught me, but there are many more to learn. The first day, as we crossed the border, the guard said, "Your smile is my antidote to a bad morning." I said, "Muchas gracias, thank you." Then I asked Chavo about "antidote." He knew, of course. It means a cure. I am already missing you.

Write back soon,
Isabel

April 9, 1957

Dear Auntie Lupita,

I forgot to tell you something. I heard Spanish being spoken in a café where we stopped on the second day of our long drive north. Then, the best part was after lunch, when we drove through many, many, *many* blue flowers. The very next day, the sky became that same blue! Chavo said, "We left a sea of blue at our feet and entered an ocean of blue over our heads." I want to talk like that.

Missing you,
Isabel

P.S. I am using my best words, and Chavo's dictionary helps with the new ones.

April 14, 1957

Dear Auntie Lupita,

    We have only been in our new home for ten days, but most of the boxes are unpacked. I like having our old things around me again. Snow came down all night and made my whole world new! This morning everything was white. I ran outside and made a snow angel. Do you remember the one we saw in the book at the library last year? Mother says it is a funny time of year for snow, and it will all melt by tomorrow. Where will the snow angel go?

                        Missing you,
                        Isabel

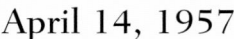

April 27, 1957

Dear Auntie Lupita,

I am sorry not to have written sooner. I started school two days after the snowstorm. My teacher is smart, like you. I think she loves teaching, like you, too! She does not speak Spanish, but she smiles at me. I am still too shy to make friends. But I have started something—a quiet place for me and my books. Father bought a big refrigerator for us and gave me the box. Now I am writing from *inside* it. Chavo cut a door in it for me. He is the best big brother a girl could have.

Missing you,
Isabel

May 18, 1957

Dear Auntie Lupita,

I am sorry if I made you sad with my last letter. This will be a happy one. Mother has started cooking for birthday parties, just like she did in Mexico. She took me with her today. The mother of the birthday girl came into the kitchen and offered me a party favor. I asked for the biggest birthday box instead. We have brought it home, and Father and Chavo are helping me make a new quiet place.

Missing you,
Isabel

June 2, 1957

Dear Auntie Lupita,

Speaking Spanish at home feels safe, but speaking English in class still feels scary. Chavo says that two languages are better than one. He is going to take a course at the college this summer. *My* classes are almost over. Mother and I are baking cakes for parties. I am getting good at beating egg whites and chopping nuts. Are you ready for a new word from me? Mother says that I am *trustworthy*. I have helped at the last two parties. There have been no big boxes. Maybe my next letter will bring good news.

Missing you,
Isabel

June 16, 1957

Dear Auntie Lupita,

I *do* have good news! No new words, but a new box. And it's a big one. Yesterday, the birthday girl was given a giant plastic pool. The box she opened was big, but not nearly as big as the pool after it was filled with air. She invited me to come out of the kitchen and splash around with everyone else. I just watched because I was wearing my dress. Then Mother helped me carry the box to our car and I smiled all the way home.

Missing you,
Isabel

July 7, 1957

Dear Auntie Lupita,

I am writing this letter from inside my quiet place. July 4th was very noisy, but the pretty fireworks were like big flowers over the lake. It was just like being back home with you. At a party last week, a girl my age was given a dollhouse and many pieces of furniture for it. Everything came in a box that is now a part of my quiet place. There are many rooms. Today Chavo said, "The colors in your house make me want to dance."

Missing you,
Isabel

August 1, 1957

Dear Auntie Lupita,

We will mail photos of my quiet place very soon. Chavo is reading the newspaper to Father while I am working on this letter. Father says that the English words are easy to understand when people talk at work, but reading is harder for him. When I get your letter every week, the Spanish words are like friends. I am learning to speak better every day, but I am getting nervous about school starting again next month. Writing to you is easier than speaking to all the new people in my life. That is because I know you love me.

Missing you,
Isabel

August 4, 1957

Dear Auntie Lupita,

Something big happened yesterday. For the first time, there was a birthday party in *our* neighborhood. After it was over, everyone clapped for us. The mother of the birthday girl said that we had made the best party ever because of the amazing cake. I also sang our birthday song from Mexico in Spanish. But there is more. Before we left, Mother invited all of the families to our house for *my* birthday! I asked them to bring me their favorite words as gifts.

Missing you,
Isabel

August 31, 1957

Dear Auntie Lupita,

Everyone came. *Everyone*. The words I liked best were: *sunrise*, *nightingale*, *twilight*, and *lullaby*, but the one I like to say out loud is *sycamore*. Mother made tamales and salsa and guacamole and beans with rice and a chocolate cake. Chavo played his guitar and Father showed the other parents some dance steps. I taught my guests our birthday song. We all sang out the windows. My quiet place was not quiet, but it didn't matter. No one wanted to go home. I hope you can feel my happiness. There is no word big enough.

Wishing you were here,
Isabel

To Abby Aceves—master chef, good friend

Farrar Straus Giroux Books for Young Readers
175 Fifth Avenue, New York 10010

Text copyright © 2012 by Sarah Stewart
Pictures copyright © 2012 by David Small
All rights reserved
Distributed in Canada by D&M Publishers, Inc.
Color separations by Embassy Graphics Ltd.
Printed in China by South China Printing Co. Ltd.,
Dongguan City, Guangdong Province
Designed by Jay Colvin
First edition, 2012
10 9 8 7 6 5 4 3 2 1

mackids.com

Library of Congress Cataloging-in-Publication Data
Stewart, Sarah, 1939–
    The quiet place / Sarah Stewart ; pictures by David Small. — 1st ed.
      p.   cm.
    Summary: A little girl moves to the United States from Mexico with her
family and writes letters to her aunt in Mexico about her new life.
    ISBN 978-0-374-32565-7
    [1. Aunts—Fiction.   2. Letters—Fiction.   3. Immigrants—Fiction.
4. Mexican Americans—Fiction.   5. Homesickness—Fiction.]   I. Small, David,
1945– ill.   II. Title.

PZ7.S84985Qu 2012
[E]—dc23
                                                        2011031768